THE PERFECT CHRISTMAS PRESENT

"I have an idea about what you can give me for Christmas," Corey said.

Jack's face lit up. "Hey, great."

"I've got this special party planned," Corey explained. "I need your help."

"No problem," said Jack. "What can I do?"

"I need you to turn off the fuse for the dining room lights at precisely six-fifteen tomorrow," she said.

Corey's Christmas Wish

BONNIE BRYANT

Illustrated by Marcy Ramsey

A SKYLARK BOOK
NEW YORK • TORONTO • LONDON • SYDNEY • AUCKLAND

RL 3, 007–010
COREY'S CHRISTMAS WISH
A Bantam Skylark Book / December 1997

Skylark Books is a registered trademark of Bantam Books,
a division of Bantam Doubleday Dell Publishing Group, Inc.
Registered in U.S. Patent and Trademark Office and elsewhere.
Pony Tails is a registered trademark of Bonnie Bryant Hiller.
"USPC" and "Pony Club" are registered trademarks of The
United States Pony Clubs, Inc., The Kentucky Horse Park,
4071 Iron Works Pike, Lexington, KY 40511-8462.

ISBN 0-553-48485-0

Published simultaneously in the United States and Canada.

Bantam Books are published by Bantam Books, a division of Bantam
Doubleday Dell Publishing Group, Inc. Its trademark, consisting of the
words "Bantam Books" and the portrayal of a rooster, is Registered in
U.S. Patent and Trademark Office and in other countries. Marca
Registrada. Bantam Books, 1540 Broadway, New York, New York
10036.

PRINTED IN THE UNITED STATES OF AMERICA

OPM   0 9 8 7 6 5 4 3 2 1

*I would like to give my special thanks
to Helen Geraghty for her help
in the writing of this book.*

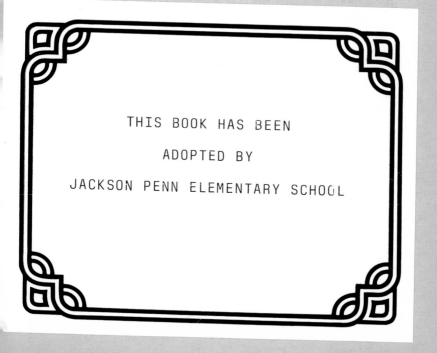

Hi, we're the **PONY TAILS**—May Grover, Corey Takamura, and Jasmine James. We're neighbors, we're best friends, and most of all, we're pony-crazy.

My name is **May**. My pony is named Macaroni after my favorite food, macaroni and cheese. He's the sweetest pony in the world! Jasmine and Corey say he's the exact opposite of me. Of course, they're just teasing. I have two older sisters who say I'm a one-girl disaster area, but they're not teasing. Would you like some used sisters? I have two for sale.

I'm called **Corey**—short for Corinne. I live between Jasmine and May—in a lot of ways. My house is between theirs. I'm between them in personality, too. Jasmine's organized, May's forgetful, and I can be both. May's impulsive, Jasmine's cautious, and I'm just reasonable. My pony is named Samurai. He's got a white blaze on his face shaped like a samurai sword. Sam is temperamental, but he's mine and I love him.

I'm **Jasmine**. My pony is named Outlaw. His face is white, like an outlaw's mask. He can be as unpredictable as an outlaw, too, but I'd never let him go to jail because I love him to pieces! I like to ride him, and I also like to look after him. I have a baby sister named Sophie. When she gets older I'm going to teach her to ride.

So why don't you tack up and have fun with us on our pony adventures! *May Corey Jasmine*

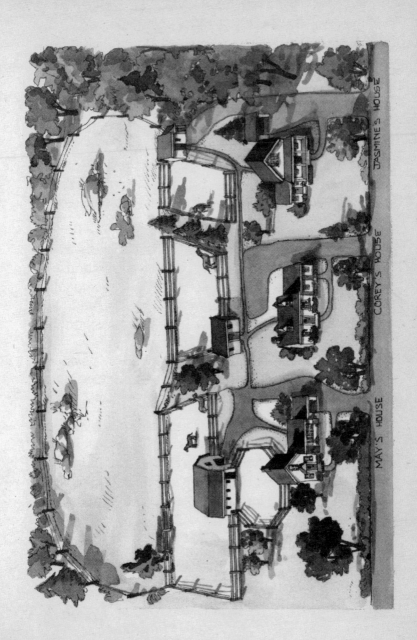

JASMINE'S HOUSE

COREY'S HOUSE

MAY'S HOUSE

Corey's
Christmas Wish

1 The Smell of Macaroni

" 'Tis the season to be jolly," May said. She pulled the book she'd just bought from the bag and looked at it with a happy sigh. The book was called *Math for Morons*. "Of course Dottie won't understand a word of it," May said happily. "It's *way* above her head." Dottie was one of May Grover's two older sisters.

May and her two best friends, Corey Takamura and Jasmine James, were Christmas shopping at the mall. The three friends called themselves the Pony Tails because they loved ponies—riding ponies, grooming ponies, everything about ponies! But holiday shopping was fun, too.

1

People rushed past with their arms full of packages. A Santa with a white beard and a red nose rang a bell. And out of the speakers came the tune of "Silent Night."

"Dottie is dumb," May sang to the music, "as dumb as they come."

"Honestly, May," said her mother. Mrs. Grover had brought the Pony Tails to the mall. "Christmas is a time for generosity and good spirits."

"My spirits are excellent," said May. "They've never been better."

Mrs. Grover shook her head, but she wore a trace of a smile.

"I love what I bought," Jasmine said. Out of her bag she pulled a tiny T-shirt with a picture of a pony on it. "I want to put Sophie in a riding mood." Sophie was her baby sister.

"Sophie's first word will be *pony*," May said.

"I'm working on it," Jasmine said with a grin. "I whisper *pony* in her ear when she's asleep."

Corey sighed. This was going to be a hard Christmas for her. It was the first one since her parents had divorced. She had been looking forward to buying presents. She had saved money from her allowance, and had planned to buy the best presents ever. But now all she could think about was that her family wouldn't be together on Christmas Day.

Corey stopped to look at a store window full of ties. There was a striped tie, but it was too formal for her father. There was a flowered one, but it was too fussy. And then there was one with horses on it.

That's it, Corey thought. That's the perfect present.

"Do you want to go in?" asked Mrs. Grover.

Corey was about to say yes when she realized that a tie is a pretty average present, even when it has horses on it. She wanted to get her father something extra-special this year.

"No thanks," she said. "It's a great tie. But . . ." She couldn't figure out how to explain.

"Why don't you give your father something really good?" asked May. "Like a

3

book on equitation?" *Equitation* was a fancy word for riding.

"That's what *you* want for Christmas," Corey said.

They passed a restaurant. A wonderful cheesy smell poured out of it. Corey had a sudden picture of a casserole of macaroni and cheese with bread crumbs on top. In her imagination, the casserole was toasty brown and the cheese was bubbling. Her father was holding the casserole and smiling.

When Corey's mother used to work late, Corey's father would make macaroni and cheese. He was a teacher of French and Spanish. He loved to pretend to be a French chef. Talking in a silly French accent, he would explain how the cheese had to be grated "just zo" and how the macaroni had to be "zoft but not too zoft" and how only the best bread crumbs would do.

Corey really missed her father. These days she often visited him at his new apartment, but that wasn't the same thing as having him at home. This *was* going to be a hard Christmas, she thought.

4

"You'll think of something," Jasmine said.

That was easy for Jasmine to say, Corey thought. Jasmine was always coming up with great ideas. At the moment, Corey's mind was a blank.

"Make something yourself," May said. "People really appreciate it when they receive something unique. Personally, I am planning to make chocolate chip cookies with cheese frosting."

"That's certainly unique," Mrs. Grover said. Corey thought she looked slightly green. May was always doing nutty things. Corey could tell that Mrs. Grover wasn't sure whether May was kidding or not.

"That's kind of understated," Jasmine said. "I would throw in a few olives."

"Good idea," said May. "And maybe a few pimientos."

"Sardines would be good," said Jasmine. "I see a sardine on top of each cookie."

"How about a pickle?" said Corey.

"Perfect," said May. "So long as it leaves room for the anchovies."

The three girls burst out laughing.

"It's a joke, isn't it?" asked Mrs. Grover.

May hugged her mother. "I'm a terrible cook. But not that terrible."

"You're a wonderful cook," Mrs. Grover said. But Corey could tell she was relieved.

"You've given me an idea," Corey said.

"Moi?" said May. *Moi* was French for "me." The Pony Tails had learned a few words of French in school that fall. It was funny, Corey thought, but the Pony Tails usually had the same idea at the same time. Here she was thinking about her father as a French chef, and May said something in French.

"I'm going to make a fabulous feast," Corey said.

"What kind of feast?" asked Jasmine.

"Macaroni and cheese," said Corey. "Is there any other kind?"

"Great choice," said May. Her pony, Macaroni, had got his name because he was the color of macaroni and cheese.

"We are needing ze zingy cheese," Corey said.

"You can't be too zingy," agreed Jasmine.

"For ze zingy cheese, I mean *the* zingy cheese, I suggest we go to Cheese World," Mrs. Grover said. "They have an excellent selection."

May linked arms with Corey and Jasmine. "Off we go to zearch for ze zingy cheese," said May.

"Zingy is the thingy," said Jasmine.

Cheese World was a madhouse, with crowds of people buying wheels of cheese and gift boxes of cheese. This didn't stop May. She marched up to a salesman and said, "Please, we would like to see some zingy cheese."

"Zingy?" said the salesman.

"I think she means something with a good strong flavor," said Mrs. Grover.

"*All* our cheeses have a good strong flavor," said the salesman.

Mrs. Grover thought for a minute. Then she said, "She means sharp."

"Would that be Limburger? Or Gorgonzola? Or Monterey Jack?" asked the salesman.

Who knew cheese had so many funny names? Corey, May, and Jasmine looked at each other with wonder.

"Is it for something in particular?" the salesman asked.

Corey looked around Cheese World. Everyone there looked so sophisticated. There were women with long coats and men in three-piece suits. There was even a boy in a three-piece suit. Corey hated to yell out *"Macaroni and cheese!"* in a spot like this.

But the salesman was waiting.

"Mcrni 'n' chse," Corey mumbled.

"I beg your pardon?" said the salesman.

Corey took a deep breath. "Macaroni and cheese." She waited for people to turn and laugh. But no one paid any attention.

"Ah, macaroni and cheese," the salesman said. "To make the best macaroni and cheese, I recommend a sharp cheddar."

"Great," said Corey. At last they were making progress.

The salesman went to a case where there were a zillion kinds of cheeses. He picked up a wheel of yellow cheese and put it on the counter. He held a knife over it. "How much would you like?" he asked.

Corey was about to say that she wanted

8

a really big chunk because she was going to make a truly cheesy casserole.

"Perhaps we could have a taste," Mrs. Grover said. She turned to the girls. "We want to make sure it has the right degree of zinginess."

With a tool shaped like a wedge, the salesman carved off four delicate curls of cheese and put them on a sheet of waxed paper. He passed the sheet to Mrs. Grover, who held it while each girl took a curl.

May was the first to try. "It tastes like a dirty foot." When the salesman looked hurt, she added, "Like a really wonderful dirty foot."

Jasmine tasted her curl of cheese. "That's interesting," she said. Jasmine was always polite.

Corey nibbled her curl of cheese. It tasted like a tin can. The salesman was watching her. Bravely she swallowed. "Er," she said, ". . . fantastic."

"Perhaps something a little milder," said Mrs. Grover.

"Would you like semi-sharp, medium, or mild?"

"Let's try mild," said Mrs. Grover.

The salesman picked up another wheel of cheese. This one looked exactly like the first one, and Corey was bracing herself for another nasty shock when the salesman handed her a curl.

She closed her eyes. She took a tiny bite, waiting for her taste buds to go into orbit. But this cheese was actually normal. "Cool," she said.

"Zingy, but not too zingy," agreed Jasmine.

"Zinginess is something you can definitely overdo," said May.

"What size wedge are you thinking of?" asked the salesman.

Corey blanked.

"How many people are going to eat the casserole?" Mrs. Grover asked helpfully.

At last, an easy question. "Three," said Corey.

Mrs. Grover looked puzzled. After all, Corey and her mother were only two people. But then Mrs. Grover shrugged.

The salesman cut a wedge of cheese that looked small. But Corey figured he knew what he was doing. He wrapped the wedge in waxed paper. Then he wrapped

10

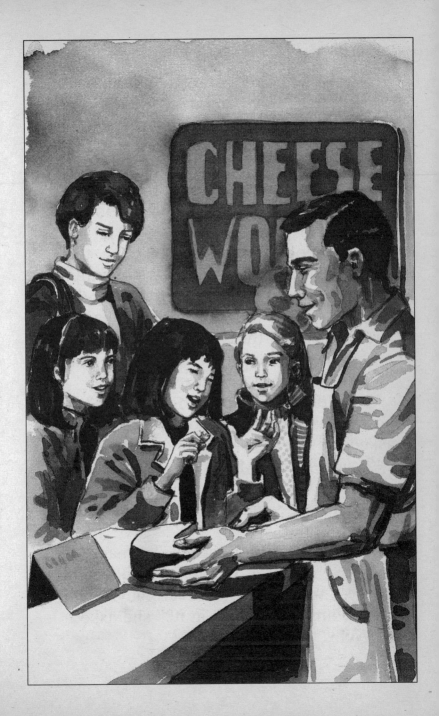

that in white paper. Then he put the package in a fancy bag and gave it to Corey.

"Now where?" said Mrs. Grover, after Corey had paid for the cheese.

"We have to get macaroni," Corey said. "I mean really excellent macaroni."

"Fancy Foods is where we want to go," Mrs. Grover said.

Fancy Foods was even crazier than Cheese World. People were running around pushing carts stacked with bottles of vinegar that had flowers in them and jars of mustard that had seeds in them.

May walked up to a clerk and said, "Show us your best macaroni."

"Would that be spinach macaroni? Or beet macaroni? Or squid ink macaroni?" asked the clerk.

"I said *best*," May said. "I didn't say *worst*."

"I think we want plain macaroni," Mrs. Grover said.

The clerk found a package of macaroni and gave it to Mrs. Grover, who gave it to Corey. Corey looked at it carefully. "Does it have anything weird in it?" she asked.

"Weird?" said the clerk.

"Like ants or something," said May.

"We have some very nice ants," the clerk said. "Chocolate covered, of course."

"That's okay," Corey said.

By the time they got out of the store, Corey was feeling pooped. Who knew that buying macaroni and cheese could be so hard?

"So there we are," said Mrs. Grover.

Corey hated to do it to Mrs. Grover and to Jasmine and May. But she wasn't finished.

"Macaroni and cheese tastes twice as good when you eat it by candlelight," she said.

"For real?" May asked.

"Absolutely," Corey said. "Otherwise macaroni and cheese is just . . . macaroni and cheese."

When they got to the candle store, Corey had lots of tough decisions to make. What color should the candles be? Should they be scented? Finally, after a lot of thought, she settled on pine-scented green candles. She figured they would look nice with macaroni and cheese.

13

"Whew," Corey said as they left the store. "Thanks for your help, guys. This is going to be a great feast."

"I'm going to dream about macaroni and cheese tonight," said May.

Corey smiled a secret smile. She had been wrong to think she never came up with ideas. She had come up with the greatest idea of all.

She was going to trick her father into coming to the feast. She would make up some kind of excuse—like that she was having trouble in school. She'd tell him that they had to have an emergency family conference. And then when her father came for the conference, she'd invite him to stay for dinner. When her father and mother were sitting at the table, she'd bring out the casserole. She'd turn off the lights. She'd light the candles, put a romantic CD in the player, and—bingo!—her parents would fall in love all over again.

2 The Animals' Christmas

"Hello," Corey said. "I'm home."

No one answered.

Corey figured that her mother was probably still in her office. Her mother, Dr. Takamura, was a veterinarian. Everybody called her Doc Tock. Her office was part of the house where she and Corey lived. Corey loved to watch her mother work, and sometimes she even got to help! As Corey headed toward the kitchen, she heard a voice upstairs and realized that her mother was on the phone.

Corey went into the kitchen and put the cheese in the refrigerator and the candles and macaroni in a cabinet. She walked into the dining room to check out the light situation. The light switch was next to the door. She realized that it would be impossible to turn off the lights without her parents' noticing.

Corey wandered into the kitchen. Over the refrigerator was the fuse box. The fuse box had switches that turned the electricity in the house on and off. If Corey could figure out a way of switching off the dining room fuse, the room would be thrown into darkness. Corey wasn't allowed to touch the fuse box. But a grown-up could. All she needed was a helpful grown-up.

On the blackboard next to the telephone she saw a note that read:

Dear Corey,
I didn't get you a Christmas present yet. Have you got any ideas?

Jack

Hmmm, Corey thought. She might have an idea. Jack was her mother's assistant. He was really nice. He'd help her. Corey poked her head into her mother's office, looking for Jack, but he wasn't there.

Corey ran upstairs.

Her mother was still on the telephone. She was saying something in a soft voice. Corey knew that voice. Her mother used it when she talked to Mr. Lee, the man she'd been dating. "That's *sooo* silly," Corey's mother said. She didn't sound as if she thought it was silly at all.

"Silly is right," Corey muttered. She stomped down the hall into her room and slammed the door.

Usually Corey loved her room. It was cozy and bright, filled with books and pictures of animals—especially ponies. Normally she'd grab a book, flop down on her bed, and read. Now none of her books looked interesting. She sat on her bed and stared at her feet.

There was a knock on her door.

"What?" Corey said.

Her mother came in. Her eyes were sparkling, and she was wearing only one earring. Corey knew that her mother always took off an earring when she talked

17

on the phone. But now it really bugged Corey.

"I'm busy," Corey said, though she wasn't busy at all.

"I have good news," her mother said.

Yes, Corey thought, Mr. Lee thinks you're wonderful.

"CARL is having an animals' Christmas party," her mother said. CARL was the County Animal Rescue League. It took care of animals that needed homes. Doc Tock gave medical care to the animals at CARL. She was on the board of directors, and so was Mr. Lee. "We want the Pony Tails to run the party."

"That's nice," Corey said.

"I thought you'd be excited," said her mother, looking disappointed.

"I am excited," Corey said. "Totally." She knew she should be happy, but she wasn't. She kept imagining her mother and Mr. Lee at the party. Probably they'd be doing something disgusting like holding hands.

"If you don't want to do it . . . ," her mother said.

Corey realized that she was acting like a

19

jerk. Her mother had been trying to make her happy. She took a deep breath and said, "It's great. It's wonderful. Thanks, Mom."

Corey's mother sighed with relief. "I knew I could count on you."

"I've got a surprise, too," Corey said.

"It's a good one, I hope," said Doc Tock.

"It's okay," said Corey with a smile. "I've decided to make MM."

"MM?" said Doc Tock, looking puzzled.

"Macaroni Madness," said Corey. "Remember how we used to have big bubbling casseroles of macaroni and cheese?"

"Yes," said Doc Tock a little sadly. "Those were fun times."

"Today at the mall I bought all the fixings," Corey said. "Gourmet cheese. Gourmet macaroni. We can have the feast before we go to the party at CARL. We can stuff ourselves first, and then stuff the animals."

"Great idea," Doc Tock said.

Her mother didn't know how great, Corey thought. Just wait! Corey was about to make her mother the happiest person on earth.

"Can I use the phone, Mom?" Corey asked.

"Of course you can use the phone," said Doc Tock. "I have the feeling you may be calling Jasmine and May."

Corey ran downstairs to the kitchen. She picked up the wall phone and hesitated. Whom should she call first, Jasmine or May? She knew it didn't really matter, but she wanted to talk to both of them at the same time.

Hey, she had the perfect solution. She called May and said, "We need to have a meeting of the Pony Tails. Can we have it in the loft in your barn first thing in the morning?"

"Great idea," said May. "I'll call Jasmine."

3 Menu Mania

The next morning Corey lay back in the hay in the Grovers' loft. From below came the steamy, earthy smell of horses. From around her came the smell of dried flowers.

May frowned. "We don't want to hurt the animals' feelings. So we have to be sure to give them equal presents."

"Those gerbils are really sensitive," said Corey with a smile. Personally, she didn't believe that the gerbils would get upset if the dogs got better presents. But she knew that May wanted to make sure every animal at CARL had a perfect Christmas.

"Folsom's has special holiday dog biscuits," said Jasmine. "They come with red and green ribbons."

"How many should we get?" asked May, her pencil poised over a sheet of paper. "We want to make sure we have enough. It would be terrible if we ran out."

They decided to get two dozen.

"How about rawhide shoes for the dogs to chew on?" said Corey.

"That would be popular, especially with the puppies," Jasmine said.

"Folsom's has Christmas ornaments made of seeds," May said.

"The birds could really get into that," said Jasmine.

"We can't forget the animals outdoors," May said. "If we give treats to the tame animals and not the wild ones, they'll be jealous."

"There's nothing worse than a jealous raccoon," said Jasmine with a giggle.

Corey wriggled farther back in the hay. To think that last week when school let out she had been dreading vacation. Everyone else had been singing and goofing and saying they'd see each other next year. But her stomach had been an empty pit. The days ahead had seemed endless.

Had she ever been wrong! This vacation was shaping up as the best ever. But Corey realized that she had one important decision left to make. She hadn't decided what music to play in the background during Macaroni Madness. Maybe, she thought, it should be something sweet and soulful like "It Came Upon a Midnight Clear." But then she thought that song was kind of slow. It was hard to chew to slow music. Maybe it should be something traditional like "The Twelve Days of Christmas." But she was kind of tired of that song. They were always playing it at the mall. Her music should be both soulful and jolly.

She had it! "Rudolf the Red-Nosed Reindeer." The song was sad because in the beginning the other animals laughed at Rudolf for having a red nose. But it was cheerful because in the end Rudolf lit up the sky with his amazing nose. If "Rudolf the Red-Nosed Reindeer" didn't bring her parents back together again, nothing would.

Earlier Corey had left a message for her father telling him that she had to talk to him. She was planning to tell him that she had missed three words on a spelling test and that her schoolwork was going right down the tubes. She *had* missed three words on a test, but it was a fifty-word test and she'd gotten the best grade in the class. She just wasn't planning to mention that.

Corey imagined her father walking into the house, looking worried and miserable, expecting to hear about her troubles in school, and then—surprise!—he'd smell the toasty casserole and hear the familiar strains of "Rudolf the Red-Nosed Reindeer." Within seconds his mood would change from anxious to joyful. Corey reminded herself that she still needed to talk to Jack to make sure he was there to turn off the fuse and plunge the dining room into darkness. But otherwise she was all set.

"Corey, have you heard one word we were saying?" asked May.

"Sure," said Corey. "Kind of."

May and Jasmine looked at each other

and shook their heads. "This is important," May said.

"Storm clouds are gathering," Jasmine said.

"What?" asked Corey. What on earth was Jasmine talking about?

"Actual storm clouds," said Jasmine. "A snowstorm is coming from up north."

"A really big one," May said. "It was on the news this morning."

"Oh," Corey said. "You mean everything will be covered with a blanket of snow?"

May nodded.

Corey smiled to herself. This Christmas was getting more and more perfect.

"It's the pits," said May grimly.

"The pits?" Corey said. "You're complaining about snow?"

"We can't go trail riding when it snows," May reminded her.

Corey realized that this was true. When it snowed, the ground became slippery. The girls weren't allowed to ride outdoors except in the Grovers' ring, which Mr. Grover kept shoveled.

"It could be months before we ride in the fields again," said Jasmine.

"Exactly," said May. "So we're going to have one last super-duper ride. I have chores to do this afternoon, and so does Jasmine. First thing tomorrow morning we'll ride in the field behind the barn."

"Yes!" Corey said.

"Afterward we'll go to Folsom's to pick up the treats for the animals," May said.

"Tomorrow is going to be one busy day," said Corey with a happy sigh.

From across the yard came the sound of May's mother calling.

"Back to earth," May said. "I'm on kitchen duty this week. I'm peeling chestnuts for the Christmas stuffing. Have you ever peeled a chestnut? I'm telling you, chestnuts are slimy."

Grumbling, May climbed down the ladder from the hayloft. Jasmine followed her, saying, "I'm stringing cranberries for the tree."

When Corey got home, there was a message for her on the blackboard next to the phone. It read, "Your dad called."

"Yes!" said Corey, pumping her fist in the air.

She was about to dial her father's number when she realized that she had better rehearse what she was going to say. She'd tell him about missing three words on the spelling test. And then she'd say she was really worried about school. And then she'd ask if he could come over the next day so that they could talk before going to the animals' Christmas party.

Corey dialed. The phone rang one, two, three, four times.

"Hello," came her father's voice on the answering machine. It sounded flat and far away. "This is 555–5976. If you'd like to leave a message, please state your name and the day and time you called."

It sounded so impersonal, as if he didn't know who was calling.

Of course he didn't know it was her, she thought. It was a recorded message.

Corey heard a beep on the machine and realized that she had to leave a message.

"It's me," Corey said. "I keep calling when you're gone. I've got this big problem. I missed three words on a spelling test. And it was a big test. I'm really worried. You miss three words, next thing you know you've missed five, then ten." She took a deep breath. The message was getting longer and longer without getting anywhere. "It's time for a family conference," she said. "How about six tomorrow?"

She put the phone down. That was, she figured, one of the dumbest phone messages ever.

Jack came into the kitchen, carrying a kitten with a bandaged tail. Usually Corey would have had a million questions about the kitten. But right now she had something else on her mind.

"I have an idea about what you can give me for Christmas," she said.

Jack's face lit up. "Hey, great."

"I've got this special party planned," Corey explained. "I need your help."

"No problem," said Jack. "What can I do?"

"I need you to turn off the fuse for the dining room lights at precisely six-fifteen tomorrow," she said.

Jack looked down at the kitten and then

29

at Corey. She could tell he was wondering what was going on.

"I don't get it," he said.

"It's kind of a joke," she said.

"Tomorrow is Kelly's birthday," Jack said. "I told her I'd take her skating at six. I hate to disappoint her." Kelly was Jack's girlfriend.

"Take her at seven," Corey said. "You can skate by moonlight."

"Then we'll miss the animals' Christmas party at CARL," Jack said.

"Go earlier in the day," Corey said.

"I have to work," Jack said. He scratched his head. "I'd really like to help you, Corey. I'll try to change my plans, but it may be hard."

4 Wild Ride

When Corey woke the next day, it was still dark. Not semi-dark, but dark, dark, dark. Trying to stay under the covers, she wiggled toward the bedside table so that she could look at the clock.

It was breakfast time. How could it be so late and still be dark? Then she remembered that two days before had been the shortest day of the year. These days the sun rose late and set early.

Corey put on a pair of blue wool breeches, a yellow sweater, and her warm riding jacket. She put on a pair of extra-heavy wool socks and roomy riding boots.

Wearing so many layers, she felt like a stuffed toy.

Jack was in the kitchen, making a pan of rice and broth for a sick animal.

"I feel really bad about this, Corey," he said. "I can't change my schedule."

"That's terrible," Corey said. "Without you my party is ruined."

"This time of year there's so much to do," Jack said with an apologetic shrug. "I'm really sorry."

"If you're too busy, you're too busy," Corey snapped.

Jack stopped stirring the rice. "What's up, Corey?"

"Nothing," she said.

"Do you want to talk?" Jack said.

"No way," she said.

Corey poured herself a bowl of granola because she knew that today she would need a lot of energy. She hunted in the refrigerator for some fruit and found a peach. She sliced it over the granola, added milk, and started eating around the edge of the bowl. This was her special way of eating cereal. May plunged into cereal any which way. Jasmine was a slow nibbler.

Corey ate a slice of peach. It was crisp. It wasn't like a juicy summer peach. But the weather outside was crisp, so it made sense for the peach to be crisp.

The phone rang.

Jack answered it. "It's your dad," he said.

Corey's stomach turned over. Great things were about to happen. She ran to the phone. "Did you get my message?"

"Kind of," her father said. "I got it, but I didn't really understand it. Since when are you having trouble in school, Corey? It doesn't sound like you."

His simple, quiet question froze her. All her stories about sinking to the bottom of the class died inside her. "Uhh," she said.

"Is it about something else?" her father asked in his gentle voice.

Corey's eyes stung with tears. "No. Yes." She could feel a howl of misery rising inside her. She swallowed to make it stop. "I thought we could have dinner. Like old times. Macaroni and cheese." She took a deep breath. Before her, as bright as if it were real, hung a picture of a bubbly casserole of macaroni and cheese. "I've got this gourmet cheese," she said. "It's zingy, but not too zingy."

"Does your mother know about this?" her father said.

Questions! Why were there so many questions?

"It's a surprise," Corey said.

There was a silence on the other end of the phone. Corey knew that her dad was thinking. Finally he said, "At a time like this . . . when things are changing . . . surprises are maybe too surprising." He cleared his throat. "If that makes any sense." Corey could see her father as clearly as if he were sitting in front of her. His dark eyes looked worried, and he was rubbing a finger on his chin, the way he did when he was upset.

"Forget it," Corey said. "Just forget it. I mean *forget* it." She slammed the phone onto the wall hook.

"Hey, Corey." Jack came over and put an arm around her. "What's going on?"

"Nothing." Corey stomped out of the kitchen into the mudroom and closed the door. There she was in the mudroom, staring at a lot of boots. That was brilliant. She opened the door and stepped outside.

She could smell the wind. It had a damp, snowy smell. Corey looked up and saw gray clouds flying southward.

Suddenly she wanted to be gone. She wanted to be far, far away. She went to the barn. Her pony, Samurai, was in his stall, half asleep. "We need a ride," she said.

Sam yawned.

Corey couldn't ride by herself. She went into the tack room and got Sam's grooming equipment. She would give Sam a long grooming while she waited for Jasmine and May.

"You are going to be the shiniest pony that ever lived," she said to Sam as she washed his hooves.

Half an hour later Sam was ready for a pony show. The only problem was that there was no show.

Corey was leaning against the side of the stall, wondering whether she should braid Sam's mane, when she heard someone outside.

"I didn't know we were going for a midnight ride," May said. Corey turned. May's jacket was buttoned wrong, and her hair was half combed. "I was sound asleep when I heard you," May said.

"It's practically lunchtime," Corey snapped. "If we don't hurry, we'll never get to Folsom's before noon."

"Errrf," said May. She looked at her watch. "I was planning to sleep late."

Jasmine appeared. She had toothpaste on her chin. Jasmine was usually very neat. Corey had never seen toothpaste on her face before.

"Am I awake, or is this a bad dream?" Jasmine groaned.

"Go back to bed," Corey said grumpily. "Enjoy your rest."

"Hey, it's a wonderful morning for a ride," May said. Corey could tell she was trying to be cheerful.

"Absolutely," said Jasmine.

"Yeah, right," Corey muttered.

May and Jasmine went to get their ponies groomed and saddled. Corey gave Sam one more grooming. He looked at her over his shoulder as if to say enough was enough.

By the time Corey got to the Grovers' paddock, May was sitting on Macaroni and Jasmine was sitting on Outlaw. All four of them looked as if they were about to go back to sleep.

"We don't have to do this," Corey said.

"Yes, we do," May said. "It's a Pony Tail pledge."

May opened the gate so that the girls could ride into the field.

Corey went first. The field was lumpy and bare with tufts of yellow grass. She passed an apple tree with withered red apples that were the only spots of color in the brown landscape.

Winter is bare, Corey thought. It's like a blanket with no fuzz on it.

On the left a broken thistle flapped in the wind. This ride wasn't making Corey feel better. It was making her feel worse.

Maybe she'd feel better if they trotted. "Want to trot?" she called. When the girls were riding without a grown-up they were allowed to trot, but they weren't allowed to go any faster.

"Why not?" called May.

"No problem," said Jasmine.

Corey pressed her knees to Sam's sides. He started to trot, but it was a slow, sleepy trot. Usually Sam arched his neck and lifted his hooves high. Now he seemed to be wondering how soon he could get back to the barn.

"Come on, Sam. Show some zip," Corey said. She touched his flanks lightly with her heels.

Sam shook his head, a sign that he was annoyed. He began to trot faster, but it wasn't his usual smooth rocking trot. He jolted from spot to spot without a steady rhythm.

"Settle down," Corey said.

Sam snorted.

"Everyone's grumpy," Corey said to herself.

Sam's left hoof caught a mound of grass and he lost his rhythm entirely, skittering forward like a chicken.

"Honestly," Corey said. "It's a good

39

thing Max can't see us." Max Regnery was the owner of Pine Hollow Stables, and the Pony Tails' riding teacher.

Sam put his head down. She could tell he was concentrating on his trot, trying to get the rhythm right. His steps got slower and slower until he was almost walking.

"Come on, Sam," Corey said. She gave him a kick.

Sam began to trot as fast as he could. It was almost like a run, with hard, fast steps.

"Hey," came May's voice from behind. "What's the rush?"

They came to a tree with dried leaves trembling on its branches. Sam trotted by without looking.

Something black and shiny and huge burst out of the tree, brushing Corey's face. She let out a yell. It was a crow. The bird flew past Sam's head, spooking him.

Sam ran. His hooves smacked the hard ground. Corey slid sideways in the saddle. She saw a pointy white rock coming at her. She pulled on Sam's mane with all her might.

She slid upright in the saddle with arms and legs flapping.

Sam whinnied with fear. He put his head down and ran all out. She could hear his breath gasping in his throat. Something blew back in her face. It was foam from his neck.

In her mind Corey could hear Max saying, "Never let a pony run too fast. You can break his wind." Corey had once seen a pony with broken wind. When he tried to gallop he made a horrible rasping sound.

"Sam!" she yelled. "Please! Please!" She knew she shouldn't be yelling. She knew she should be calm and self-assured. But she was too scared.

The ground was a silvery blur. She felt as if she were flying into the clouds.

All she could hear was the steady thudding of her bottom on the saddle and the rattle of Sam's breath.

Tears streamed out of the corners of her eyes. She felt like sobbing. But in her mind she saw Max's bright blue eyes. She could see him nodding. Max was telling her she could do it.

Corey forced her hands to unclench.

She forced her back to unfreeze. She tried to ride with Sam and not against him.

"It's okay, Sam," she said.

Her words were blown back in the wind. Sam couldn't hear her. But he must have felt a change. There was a sigh inside his gallop. Something eased.

Corey put her heels down and her wrists up. Sam was still galloping, but she could feel his muscles relaxing. Without being asked, he slowed to a canter. Corey rose in the stirrups so that her bottom was a couple of inches off the saddle.

Sam moved down to a trot, and then to a walk. Corey looked back. May and Jasmine were tiny shapes against the gray sky.

"Did I hurt you, Sam?" asked Corey as the pony came to a halt.

She climbed down and went around to Sam's head. There was foam around his lips, and his neck was flecked with white.

"Sam," she said. "Oh, Sam." She put her arms around his neck. She could feel his heart booming.

"Oh, boy," she said into his mane. "Oh, sweetie."

She heard hoofbeats. Jasmine and May rode up.

"Are you okay?" May said.

"Check Sam," Corey said. "He's what counts."

May and Jasmine tied their ponies to trees and came over to examine Sam. May checked his legs. Jasmine listened to his breathing.

"I'm not a vet," May said. "But he looks okay to me."

"His breathing seems okay to me," Jasmine said.

"Corey, you scared the wits out of me," May said.

"I scared the wits out of myself," Corey said.

May and Jasmine hugged Corey. Then they hugged Sam.

May checked her watch. "We still have time to get to Folsom's."

"Yes!" said Jasmine.

"Whew," said Corey.

They got onto their ponies. They had to walk because Sam had had enough action for one day.

When they got home, they untacked the ponies and hopped onto their bikes.

As they turned into the road, Corey felt something on her nose. She looked up. Snowflakes were drifting down. She stuck out her tongue and felt the sting of the first flake. She looked at May and Jasmine and grinned.

But when they got to Folsom's she stopped grinning. There was a sign on the door that read:

CLOSED EARLY BECAUSE OF SNOW.
HAVE A HAPPY HOLIDAY.

"There goes the animals' Christmas," groaned Corey.

5 The Three Chefs

The three of them headed miserably home.

"I can't do anything right," Corey said.

"Oh, come on," May said. "It's not that bad."

"You don't know," said Corey gloomily. She told them how she had tried to trick her father into coming for dinner. And how he wasn't coming. And how she was stuck with all this macaroni and cheese that no one wanted to eat. And how her father thought she was a dork.

And now the animals had nothing to eat.

"I ruined Christmas," Corey said.

46

"You did not," said Jasmine.

"You didn't ruin it. You just injured it slightly," said May with a giggle. "Besides, I have an idea."

"Not even you can fix this mess," said Corey.

"Remember how we convinced my mother that we were going to make the world's scariest cookies?" May said.

Corey nodded.

"What if we make the world's *best* cookies?" May said. "And biscuits and chewies? What if we make a great animal feast?"

"How are we going to do that?" asked Corey.

"Our feed room is full of things that animals love to eat," May said. "Like oats and apples."

"But that's not special," Corey said. "It's everyday food, not party food."

"Says who?" said May indignantly. "As of this moment the Pony Tails are great chefs. When we get through, the party will be an extravaganza. The animals will be talking about it for years to come. Parakeets will tell their grandchildren

47

about it. Raccoons will bear the word until the Pony Tails are famous from one end of Willow Creek to the other."

"I could go for that," said Jasmine, laughing. "I am totally unknown among raccoons."

"We'll fix that," May said.

They went to the Grovers' house, and May asked her father for permission to take feed from the feed room. When Mr. Grover heard that it was for the animals' Christmas at CARL, he said they could take as much as they wanted.

May insisted on taking buckets of everything.

"This is just for one meal, not all year," protested Jasmine as she lugged one of the heavy buckets.

"You'd be amazed at how the animals will gobble our fantastic treats," May said.

"I think Mom has a recipe for home-made dog biscuits," Corey said. "She can help us."

But when they went to Corey's house, it turned out that Doc Tock was at the animal hospital in Willow Creek, taking care of a sick dog.

"Your mother left a message for you," May said. She pointed to the blackboard in the kitchen next to the refrigerator. On it Doc Tock had written:

Dear Corey, I can't wait for Macaroni Madness tonight.

Love,
Mom

"Yerrrch," said Corey, clutching her head. The thought of the meal filled her with horror.

"Wait a second," May said. "You can take it."

"I can?" said Corey.

"You know it," Jasmine said. "Pony Tails are strong."

"And brave," said May. "Pony Tails aren't afraid of macaroni and cheese."

"I'm not so sure," said Corey. The thought of that casserole made her quiver and quake.

"Always remember that you're a Pony Tail," Jasmine said.

"I'll try," said Corey.

"On to Jasmine's house," said May.

49

When they got to Jasmine's house, Mrs. James was sitting in the kitchen with a cup of tea. "Can you believe it? Sophie is asleep and I've got a moment to myself," she said.

"There's nothing worse than a moment to yourself," May said darkly.

"Really?" said Mrs. James with a smile. "I've been dreaming about it for weeks."

"You could get bored," May said quickly.

"I don't feel bored," Mrs. James said.

"Boredom leads to trouble," May said. "You could wind up getting arrested or something."

"Oh," said Mrs. James. "I hadn't thought of that."

"Luckily, we have just the solution for your free-time problem," May said. "We are going to make treats for the animals' Christmas party at CARL, and we need you to help us."

Corey winced. She figured that the last thing Mrs. James wanted was to fuss around in the kitchen. But, to her amazement, Mrs. James smiled.

"That's just what I would like to do,"

Mrs. James said. "I haven't done a project with the Pony Tails in ages."

"We want to make really great things," Jasmine said. "Nothing ordinary."

"Hmmm," said Mrs. James. "I have a few ideas."

The Pony Tails grinned at each other. Not only was Mrs. James a great cook, but she was an artist, too.

Mrs. James came back from the sewing room, where she kept her crafts supplies. Her arms were full of papers.

"I have a recipe for dog biscuits," she said.

"We'll make two sizes," said May, her eyes wide with excitement. "Puppy Pops and Dog Divines."

Mrs. James smiled. Corey could tell that she *was* glad to be back at work with the Pony Tails.

"I have a recipe for Christmas bells made of bird seed. We could hang them in the trees for the wild birds," said Mrs. James

"We'll call them Wild Bird Bells," said Corey.

"We need red ribbon to tie the bells to

51

the trees," Jasmine said. She dashed off to Mrs. James's sewing room to get some.

"I have a recipe here for liver treats for cats," Mrs. James said.

"Liver, *yeeeeeu*," said May.

"Phew," said Corey. All three Pony Tails were nuts about liver. That is, it drove them nuts.

"But if cats want liver, we'll give them liver. In fact, we'll give them Cat Candy!" said May. "Isn't that what Christmas is all about?"

By the end of the afternoon the Pony Tails had baskets of colorful Christmas treats for the animals at CARL. Nothing was left except for some dried flowers and a bowl of tiny lady apples.

"Wait a second," May said. "What about our ponies? Let's make treats for them." Then they turned the dried flowers and lady apples into fancy bouquets.

"These are Pony Perfections," May said.

The girls packed the CARL treats in the back of the Jameses' station wagon, and they left the Pony Perfections in the Jameses' mudroom, next to the kitchen.

Mrs. James looked at her watch. "It's time for dinner."

Corey's stomach turned over. It was time for her and her mother to have Macaroni Madness.

6 Macaroni Misery

Talk about bad ideas, Corey thought. Macaroni Madness was up there with the worst ideas of mankind.

As Corey walked into the mudroom of her house, she repeated to herself what May had told her—the Pony Tails were strong, and they were brave. They could handle anything, even macaroni and cheese.

From the kitchen came the sound of her mother talking on the telephone. "Everyone will be so excited," her mother said. She was using the happy voice she used when she talked to Mr. Lee.

Corey stood still. She knew that she

shouldn't listen to her mother's conversation. But her feet were stuck to the floor.

"It's so perfect," Doc Tock said. "I can't wait until the announcement."

Corey had a sudden thought. What if her mother and Mr. Lee were talking about getting married? What if they were going to announce their engagement at the animals' Christmas party?

Corey thought of all the food the Pony Tails and Mrs. James had made. For a second she wished they hadn't made it. What's to celebrate? she thought. Then she realized that she was being a jerk again.

She put her chin up and said to herself, "I'm a Pony Tail. I can take it."

Corey walked into the kitchen wearing a big grin. The grin felt absolutely phony, but at least it was there.

"Hi," Doc Tock said happily. "My stomach is growling. Let's get started on our Macaroni Madness."

"No problem," Corey said. She marched over to the refrigerator and got out the cheddar cheese. "We grate the cheddar cheese very fine."

"I'll do that," her mother said.

"For the macaroni we need a huge pot of boiling water," Corey said. "You don't want to crowd your macaroni."

"No way," her mother said. Doc Tock settled happily at the kitchen table to grate the cheese. "There's going to be a wonderful surprise tonight," she said.

"I can't wait," Corey muttered.

"You'll be thrilled," Doc Tock said.

"I'm thrilled already," Corey said grimly.

While she was waiting for the water to boil, Corey set the dining room table. She used Christmassy green mats, jolly red plates, and the best silver. She stood back to look. The table was definitely missing something.

Candles. With a heavy heart Corey walked back into the kitchen to get the candles.

"Your water's boiling," her mother said.

Corey got the macaroni from the cabinet, opened the pack, and held it over the water. Here goes nothing, she thought. She dumped the macaroni into the boiling water.

"I love that smell," her mother said.

"Wait until the casserole is baking and bubbling," Corey said bravely. "Then you'll really smell something great."

Corey got the candles and pulled off the cellophane wrapping.

"What lovely candles," Doc Tock said. "You have great ideas, Corey."

Corey took the candles out to the dining room and put them in candlesticks. That's me, Corey thought, a fountain of bad ideas.

7 Oh Come, All Ye Parakeets

"Goober the skinny greyhound had a very clammy nose," sang May to the tune of "Rudolf the Red-Nosed Reindeer." The Pony Tails were in the Jameses' station wagon on the way to the animals' Christmas party.

"Come on, Corey," May said. "We've got to practice." May had written Christmas songs to sing to the animals at the party.

"I'm not in the mood," Corey said.

"You don't like that song? Then we'll sing 'Oh Come, All Ye Parakeets,'" said May. To the tune of "Oh Come, All Ye Faithful" May sang:

"Oh come, all ye parakeets,
Joyful and triumphant!"

Corey knew she was supposed to join in, but she couldn't.

"You've got to practice, Corey," said May.

"I'll fake it," said Corey glumly.

The station wagon headed down a road with bare maple trees on either side. It pulled up in a parking lot that was jammed with cars.

"CARL has a big crowd," said Mrs. James.

Great, Corey thought, everyone in Willow Creek will be here for the engagement announcement.

"Who knew so many people would come?" said May. She sounded a little awed. But then she said, "Lucky them—they get to hear us sing."

Jasmine collapsed into giggles. But Corey felt worse than ever. This was like being in a horror movie.

"I see your mother, Corey," Mrs. James said. "She's by the front door."

Corey spotted her mother. She was

61

wearing silver earrings and a silver pinecone pin on her collar. Next to her was Mr. Lee. They both looked very happy, which made Corey feel even worse.

May jumped out of the car and did a rock-and-roll dance. "It's snoooowing," she sang.

Corey got out and looked up. The snow was white and powdery.

"Yo ho ho and a barrel of snow," sang May.

"Are you okay?" said Jasmine softly to Corey.

Corey swallowed. "Kind of."

Jasmine put her arm around Corey.

Next thing Corey knew, May had her arm around her, too. "Hey," May said. "What's up?"

Corey nodded toward her mother and Mr. Lee. "I think they're going to announce their engagement," she whispered.

"Oh, man," May whispered.

"We can handle it," Jasmine whispered.

"No, we can't," whispered Corey.

"Yes, we can. We're the Pony Tails," said May.

Corey's chin went up. She didn't really believe that she could handle it, but she knew she had to try.

Holding hands, the Pony Tails stood at the back of the crowd.

Mr. Lee stepped to the microphone. "Welcome to this happy event," he said.

May and Jasmine squeezed Corey's hands even harder.

"This has been the most outstanding year in the history of CARL," Mr. Lee said. He went on to tell how many cats, dogs, birds, gerbils, rabbits, and white mice CARL had saved.

Who else could make pets sound boring? Corey thought. She imagined Mr. Lee at the breakfast table making lists of all the things he was going to do that day.

Corey felt an elbow in her ribs and saw that May and Jasmine were smiling and waving to the crowd. Mr. Lee was saying, "And now Corey Takamura, May Grover, and Jasmine James will feed the animals."

The girls uncovered the baskets that held the animal treats. The crowd oohed and aahed.

Corey spotted her father over at the side. If only he didn't have to be here.

"Heads up," whispered May.

Corey put her chin so far up that her neck ached.

They went inside the shelter, with Mr. Lee and everyone else following. May explained about the Cat Candy, Puppy Pops, Dog Divines, and Wild Bird Bells.

"You girls have done a wonderful job," Mr. Lee said. "The animals will really love their treats."

Corey thought the animals did look pretty happy.

"And now the girls are going outside to feed the wild animals," said Mr. Lee. "It was their idea."

The crowd murmured with approval.

When everyone went outside, the Pony Tails spread Deer Dessert on the hillside and hung Wild Bird Bells from the trees. They scattered Chipmunk Chewies around the bushes and Mouse Munchies next to the walk.

"As soon as we leave, the wild animals will have their own feast," Mr. Lee said. He cleared his throat. "Soon I will be making an important announcement. But first the girls have some songs to sing."

"No songs," Corey whispered.

"We can do it," Jasmine whispered. "We're the Pony Tails."

From her pocket May pulled three sheets with the words to the songs on them. "Which one should we start with?" May said.

"Let's go for the parakeets," said Corey bravely.

The Pony Tails held up their sheets, put up their chins, and sang:

"Oh come, all ye parakeets,
Joyful and triumphant!
Come ye, oh come ye to
the Animal Rescue League.
Come and behold them.
See the happy gerbils.
See the chipmunk family . . ."

That did it. Corey felt a sob rise within her. She looked up. The snow was falling faster. Through her tears the snowflakes looked like stars.

8 Silent Snow

When they were done, Mr. Lee pulled out his handkerchief and blew his nose. "That was beautiful," he said, looking puzzled by his emotional response. He put the handkerchief back in his pocket. "And now for the important announcement we've been talking about."

Doc Tock stepped forward with a big grin on her face. She winked at Corey.

For a second Corey almost hated her mother. Corey shrank into the crowd. If she could make herself invisible, maybe she wouldn't hear Mr. Lee's big announcement.

"This year CARL is going to do something it has never done before," Mr. Lee said. "It is going to award a prize for outstanding work with animals. I guess it's pretty obvious who gets the prize." There was a murmur from the crowd. "The winners are Jasmine James, May Grover, and Corey Takamura. Not only did they organize this wonderful party, but all year they have been helping feed and groom the animals. They've made a lot of lonely dogs and cats feel better."

"Oh," said Corey.

May nudged her.

"Wow," Corey said.

May flashed a grin and said, "This is the greatest thing ever."

"It sure is," said Jasmine.

"That's it?" Corey whispered. "That's all?"

"Yes," whispered May.

The crowd cheered. Doc Tock stepped forward, put her arms around Corey, and hugged her. Corey hugged her back as hard as she could. May's and Jasmine's parents hugged them, too.

"Speech!" called the crowd.

Corey looked at May because May was

great at making speeches. But May shook her head. "You do it," she said.

Smiling, Mr. Lee handed Corey a silver cup with the names of the three Pony Tails engraved on it.

What do I do now? Corey thought. But then she remembered that at the Academy Awards people always hold up their Oscars. She held up the cup so that everyone could see it.

For a second Corey watched snow falling on the beautiful cup. But then she realized that everyone was waiting for her to make a speech.

"This is a big surprise," Corey said. "I mean *really* big." Beside her Jasmine and May were grinning. "It makes me think of Christmas presents. When you open your presents, they're never what you expect. They're better."

Corey thought that was a pretty good speech. But then she realized that people were waiting for more. She tried to remember what winners said when they accepted Academy Awards. She remembered that they always thanked a million people. "I'd like to thank my parents,"

Corey said. Her father had come up out of the crowd. He was standing next to her mother, and both of them were beaming. Her parents turned and smiled at each other. It was the smile of friends.

"I'd like to thank Max Regnery of Pine Hollow Stables," Corey said. Max stepped out of the crowd, his blue eyes gleaming. "Max has taught us more than we can ever tell."

"And finally," Corey said, "I'd like to thank May Grover and Jasmine James, who are the two best friends on earth."

Next thing Corey knew, everybody was shaking her hand, patting her on the back, and taking her picture. She grinned at May and Jasmine. It was like being a star.

Mr. Lee came up to Corey with a camera. "How about a picture of you and your mother?" Somehow Mr. Lee didn't seem so horrible now.

"No problem," Corey said. She put an arm around her mother.

Mr. Lee turned to Corey's father. "How about a picture of the three of you?"

Corey was astounded. Her father and Mr. Lee didn't hate each other. Her father smiled and said he thought that was a great idea.

Then Corey had her picture taken with Mr. Lee and her mother. At first the idea made her nervous. But then it felt okay. She took another look at Mr. Lee. Maybe he wasn't so bad. And he certainly made her mother happy.

She had her picture taken with her first-grade teacher. And with Jack, her mother's assistant. And with Kelly, Jack's girlfriend.

Corey realized that being a star was a tough job. You could get a smile-ache.

Finally Doc Tock said, "Corey, you look tired. It's time to head home."

"Great idea!" said Corey. "We can show the cup to the ponies. They'll be proud."

"I'm sure they will," said Doc Tock with a smile. She turned to May and Jasmine. "Would you like to come with us? It looks like your parents are busy." Mr. Grover was talking to someone who wanted him to train a horse. And Mrs. James was talking to the art teacher at the Willow Creek school.

"Absolutely," said May. "The ponies have got to hear about this."

In the car on the way home the Pony Tails didn't say a thing. They snuggled together, feeling happy and close. When Doc Tock drove the car into the garage, they jumped out and ran to Corey's stable to see Samurai.

"You won't believe what happened," Corey said to Sam. "I thought my mother was engaged, but she wasn't engaged, and there was this whole big crowd, and we fed the animals, and then we had to sing this silly song. And I nearly cried. And then we became world famous. But otherwise, it was a kind of boring night."

"Too bad you didn't hear us sing," said May to Sam.

"You really missed something," said Jasmine.

"Maybe we should sing for Sam," said May.

"That's okay," Corey said. "I don't want him to have nightmares."

On the other side of the stable door the snow was falling harder now.

"It's going to snow all night," Jasmine said. "I heard it on the radio."

"I have an idea," said May.

"Ho boy," said Corey and Jasmine together.

"This is a good one," May said. "We haven't given the ponies their Christmas treats."

"How could we forget?" said Corey, slapping her forehead.

"And this is the first snow," May said. "They love snow. Or anyway I do, and that's good enough for me."

"Yes?" said Corey, wondering what May had in mind.

"Why don't we take the ponies outside and let them eat their treats in the snow?" asked May.

"Wow," said Corey. "That is an excellent idea."

Jasmine went to her house to get the treats. When she came back, the girls led their ponies into the Grovers' paddock. It was snowing heavily now, and the paddock was blanketed with white.

The girls put the bouquets on top of the snow. The ponies began to munch.

There was no sound except for the noise of the ponies chewing and the gentle hush of falling snow.

"I got my wish," Corey said softly. "I wanted the best Christmas ever, and this is it."

"It's my best, too," said Jasmine.

"Mine, too," said May.

Corey looked at the row of houses—hers, May's, and Jasmine's. They were so bright and warm and cozy. She looked at the dark, jagged line of the trees against the sky. "Next year is going to have good things and bad things," Corey said. "Adventures and . . ."

"Catastrophes," said May.

"But we'll be together," Jasmine said.

They put their arms around each other so that they made a ring. They leaned together, their heads touching. Corey felt snowflakes prickling the back of her neck.

Something was poking her. She turned to look. Sam was done eating, and he wanted to get into the circle. She pulled

him into the circle. Jasmine and May pulled in Outlaw and Macaroni.

The Pony Tails and their ponies stood in a circle as snow settled on their heads. Corey said what they were all thinking: "We're the best six friends on earth."

COREY'S TIPS ON PONY SNACKS

I sometimes joke that my favorite class in school is lunch. It's no joke at all that Sam's favorite time of the day is feeding time. No, that's not quite true. He loves his meals, but what he loves the best is snacks. If he could talk, he'd tell me he wants a lump of sugar every time I pat him. I could give him all that sugar, but it wouldn't be good for him.

Snacks are important for ponies (just as they are for the ponies' riders). And because they are important, there are two things I always have to be careful about with Sam's snacks: *what* I give him and *when* I give it to him.

The *what* part is the same sort of thing your parents say to you about snacks. Snacks shouldn't just be empty calories. When my taste buds say, "Sticky, gooey, cream-filled baked thing!", my mother says "Apple!" She's right, too. The bakery treat doesn't have any vitamins, but it does have lots of fat, which my body doesn't need, and loads of refined sugar, which doesn't stick around long enough to give me much energy. It just stays with me long enough to wreck my appetite for dinner. The apple has all kinds of vitamins and minerals in it, plus natural, un-processed sugar, which I need for energy. I also like raisins, peaches, oranges, and plums, and my favorite is celery with pea-nut butter. I don't like apricots, but that's just me. And every once in a while, I really want a bakery treat. That's okay, too. Ev-ery once in a while.

It's the same thing with horses. Samurai would be only too happy to have a constant supply of sugar lumps. It doesn't do him any more good than the bakery treats do me. He needs things that he likes that will improve his diet, not ruin his appetite. (I sound more and more like my mother every day—and I'm only eight!)

In fact, ponies need a lot of the good things they can get from snack foods. Carrots are especially good for them because they've got body builders that ponies sometimes can't get anywhere else except in special feed mixes. I keep a bag of carrots in the refrigerator, marked "Sam," so that it's always there when I go out to the stable. I also chop up carrots and put them into Sam's morning feed mix. He likes carrots so much that they make him not notice some of the things he's not so crazy about in his feed.

I usually give him a carrot when I finish a ride or a workout with him and after he's been particularly well behaved as I groom him. He gets a carrot when the farrier gives him a new set of shoes (that is, *if* he behaves). I use carrots as rewards.

Sam gets other things besides carrots. I

know this sounds funny, but he loves pumpkin! When I buy my Halloween pumpkin, Mom and I always pick up an extra for Sam. I cut it into small pieces, and he just gobbles it! He also likes turnips and parsnips. That's a good thing, because I *hate* them. If Mom is making turnips for dinner, I always tell her that we have to share with Sam, and I give him a big share (cut up and raw) so that I'll get a smaller share (cooked and mashed). That's just one of the nice things about having a pony.

Sometimes he enjoys a little snack of lettuce, or any greens. He's welcome to all those things, in small portions. He can also have apples. Ponies love apples. They're sweet and juicy, but it's a good idea to limit the apples a pony gets. Two is enough in any one day for a full-sized horse. I limit Sam's apple eating to one a day. The thing about apples is that they can affect a pony's digestive system, and ponies have very fussy stomachs. The last thing I want is to have Sam get colicky because of a treat I gave him!

Now, the other thing I have to tell you is that it matters *when* I give Sam treats, and this is true for every pony in the world. If an owner gives a pony a treat every time she sees him, the pony expects a treat every time his owner shows up. He'll nuzzle her pockets, reach for her hands with his nose, and try to sniff where the treat is. This can be cute once. It tickles, and the owner laughs. Maybe she'll laugh the second time it happens. But when it becomes a habit, it happens *every* single time. The pony doesn't want to do anything until he gets his treat. He can become balky, feisty, and moody. What he's learned is that he's supposed to get a treat before anything else happens. Wrong!

The solution to that is that you only ever give treats as a reward. If your pony has done something right, let him know. Pat him, talk softly to him, cluck your tongue to him. It makes him feel good when you feel good. And sometimes you can give him a treat, too. That makes him feel even better. He knows he's earned it. That will get you a well-behaved pony, and a well-behaved pony deserves lots of treats. As long as they're healthy treats, you've done two good things for him.

Oh, and every once in a while, Sam gets a sugar lump. He likes it, and it reminds me that it's probably time to ask my mom for a gooey bakery treat.

About the Author

Bonnie Bryant was born and raised in New York City, and she still lives there today. She spends her summers in a house on a lake in Massachusetts.

Ms. Bryant began writing about girls and horses when she started The Saddle Club series in 1987. So far there are more than seventy books in that series. Much as she likes telling the stories about Stevie, Carole, and Lisa, she decided that the younger riders at Pine Hollow Stables, especially May Grover, have stories of their own. That's how Pony Tails was born.

Ms. Bryant rides horses when she has time away from her computer, but she doesn't have a horse of her own. She likes to ride different horses, enjoying a variety of riding experiences. She thinks most of her readers are much better riders than she is!

Don't miss Bonnie Bryant's next Pony Tails adventure . . .

JASMINE AND THE JUMPING PONY
Pony Tails #16

Jasmine James is thrilled at the thought of taking her first real jumping class at Pine Hollow Stables. She and her pony, Outlaw, have done some jumping before, but now they're going to learn the correct way to get over those fences. During her very first lesson, Jasmine makes a mistake, and her pony stumbles. Jasmine falls, but she isn't hurt. She is, however, scared—very scared. She's so upset that she says she'll never jump again, ever! Now May and Corey have to convince Jasmine to give her pony, and herself, another chance.

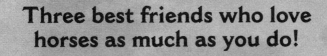

Saddle Up For Fun!
Join The Saddle Club

As an official Saddle Club member you'll get:

- *Saddle Club newsletter*
- *Saddle Club membership card*
- *Saddle Club bookmark*
- *and exciting updates on everything that's happening with your favorite series.*

Bantam Doubleday Dell Books for Young Readers
Saddle Club Membership Box BK
1540 Broadway
New York, NY 10036

SKYLARK

Bantam Doubleday Dell
Books for Young Readers

Name _____

Address _____

City _____ **State** _____ **Zip** _____

Date of birth _____

Offer good while supplies last.

BFYR - 8/93

THYROID PROBLEMS IN WOMEN
AND CHILDREN

DATE DUE

AUG 1 2 2004		
OCT 2 7 2004		
APR 2 1 2005		

DEMCO 38-296

Ordering

Trade bookstores in the U.S. and Canada please contact:

Publishers Group West
1700 Fourth Street, Berkeley CA 94710
Phone: (800) 788-3123   Fax: (510) 528-3444

Hunter House books are available at bulk discounts for textbook course adoptions; to qualifying community, health-care, and government organizations; and for special promotions and fund-raising. For details please contact:

Special Sales Department
Hunter House Inc., PO Box 2914, Alameda CA 94501-0914
Phone: (510) 865-5282   Fax: (510) 865-4295
E-mail: ordering@hunterhouse.com

Individuals can order our books from most bookstores, by calling **(800) 266-5592**, or from our website at **www.hunterhouse.com**